MW00936215

"Another great Bella novella. I love these books. I have fallen in love with Bella and DJ and their families. I feel like I am part of their family. The characters all seem so real and I love the humor that is also part of the book. It is well written and I can't wait to read the next one in the series."

—WILANI WAHL, REGARDING *THE TENDER TRAP*

"Bella Rossi is one of my all-time favorite characters in a contemporary romantic comedy, and Janice Thompson is at the top of my list when it comes to must read fiction! When I found out she was writing a series of stories called The Bella Novella Collection, I had them on my wish list before you could say Dean Martin!"

—DEENA PETERSON, READER

"I'm pretty sure Bella is my favorite book character of all time, and I was more than excited to find out Janice Thompson has brought us back into her life. Bella is back to doing what she does best - pulling off impossibly perfect wedding ceremonies. We also get to connect with DJ and the rest of Bella's crazy family."

—KAREN, READER

"Bella never fails to capture the reader's attention and pull you in to the chaos of the Rossi family all the while leading you to the One who makes order out of our chaos. Can't wait to read the next installment."

—MCKINSEY JONES, READER

"Bella and the Rossi clan are back and I couldn't be happier! I was so happy to read this book and felt like I was among old friends again....even the Splendora Sisters are back! This is a must read and if you haven't read the other Bella books by Janice Thompson, go grab them right now and get to reading them. They are ALL wonderful. Janice is one of my very favorite authors because I love Christian fiction and she knows how to write it."

—AMAZON READER

"Mama Mia, let's escape! Let's fall in love! Let's eat Chicken Parmesan, Fettuccine Alfredo, and Bubba's down-home barbecue without gaining a pound. It's all possible when we hang out with Bella Rossi! You'll root for the Rossi and Neeley families as they break down cultural barriers and rush toward each other, arms wide open."

—TRISH PERRY, AUTHOR, *BEACH DREAMS* AND
THE GUY I'M NOT DATING

The Bella Novella Collection

Book Five

The Tender Trap

JANICE THOMPSON

The Tender Trap
Copyright © 2017 by Janice Thompson.

Printed in the United States of America.

DEDICATION

To all of my single author-friends: Our day is coming.

Chapter One

A TALE OF TWO CITIES

"Oh boy. Oh boy, oh boy, oh boy."

I stared at the front of the Rosenberg Library, not far from my home in Galveston, and tried to give myself a little pep talk before going inside to meet up with my latest bride and groom. When the only words that wanted to emerge were "Oh boy," I knew I was in trouble.

I'd coordinated a zillion weddings, so why the nerves? I rarely sweated over meeting with potential brides and grooms. But this couple? Well, they were a horse of a different color. Or, to be more specific, a literary duo of a different color.

My phone calls with the bride, Elizabeth, had been interesting, to say the least. The bookish literature professor had over-the-top library-esque ideas for her big day and I'd promised to come through for her. But I'd never coordinated a book-themed ceremony before, so I hardly knew where to start. For that matter, I barely remembered the novels I'd read in high school, so how could I even pretend to understand her heartfelt passion for the classics? Incorporating them into her mid-November wedding would take some work.

And the groom? Walter? Ack. That guy gave me the

shivers. Okay, so he had his own pop psychology radio show. I'd tried to listen in, but. . .really? His arrogance made me want to smack someone. And what was up with the title of his latest book: *I'm Okay, You Need Some Work*? Did he really think people would be won over by that?

"Oh boy, oh boy, oh boy."

Out of the corner of my eye I caught a glimpse of the bride and groom-to-be as they exited his sleek black Porsche. She had wound her long, dark hair into a casual bun, of sorts, and had used a pencil to hold it in place. Interesting.

The groom? He looked to be a younger and somewhat hipper version of Dr. Phil. The casual jacket and lack of tie made him seem a bit more approachable, but my recent phone calls with the guy begged to differ. To call him a diva would be putting it mildly.

"Oh boy."

I checked my appearance in the rearview mirror, sent a quick note to my husband, D.J. who was still mourning the recent loss of our dog, Precious, and then grabbed my laptop. Might as well get this over with. With a plastered smile on my face, I climbed out of my vehicle and strode their way, doing all I could to appear confident. Either the groom wasn't buying it or he was in a mood. The corners of his mouth remained in a downturned position as he greeted me with a curt nod.

Still, I stuck out my hand and gave them my version of a professional nod. "Afternoon, you two. Ready to set some plans in motion."

"Indeed." He countered my nod with a stiff up and down motion of his head.

"Bella, I'm so excited!" The beautiful Elizabeth reached over and grabbed my hand, her hair shimmering in the October sunlight. "I think we've hit on something here. Our guests are going to be thrilled."

"Well, as I said on the phone, I've never done a book-themed wedding before, so it will be a first for me. But I feel sure we can work together to pull off your dream ceremony and reception."

I hoped.

The "humph" from the groom did little to squelch my nerves.

Oh boy.

"We wanted to bring you to the Rosenberg library to give you a little glimpse into our world." Elizabeth released a girlish sigh and gestured with her head to the grand building in front of us. "I. Just. Love. The. Smell. Of. Books. Don't you, Bella?"

"Me?" Well, I loved the smell of manicotti. And lasagna. And my Uncle Laz's Mambo Italiano pizza from the family restaurant, Parma Johns. But, books? Really? "I, um, never thought about it before."

She turned toward building, a look of bliss on her face. Then she grabbed my hand. "Follow me inside and you're bound to fall in love."

Should I tell her that I was already in love—with my East Texas cowboy—that long tall drink of water, D.J.? And with our four children, Tres, little Rosie, and the twins? Should I tell her that I'd already fallen head-over-heels with the little one safely tucked away in my womb for the next four months? Nah, I'd let all of that ride.

I tagged along on her heels up the front stairs to the library. Elizabeth opened the front door and Walter shot in ahead of me. D.J. would've flipped. This guy might be a famous pop psychologist, he might have his own radio show, but he didn't even open a door for his bride-to-be or the pregnant wedding coordinator? Ugh.

I subtracted ten points right away from his original score of 70, which I'd mentally assigned him after our last phone call. Hopefully he wouldn't give me any other reasons to do math today.

From the minute we stepped inside the library, I felt swallowed alive by books. Sure, I'd been here before, even brought the kids. But something about entering this sacred place with these two literary-types felt confining. Could a person die from breathing in too many books? I wondered, as I tugged at the neckline of my sweater.

"Oh, smell that!" Elizabeth clutched her hands to her chest and a look of pure delight settled on that pretty face of hers. "I *love* that smell!"

Smelled musty to me, but I'd never say so. Still, I'd never seen such bliss in a person's eyes over books before. Sort of the same look I saw on D.J.'s face every time his brother Bubba barbecued. Or the look in the customers' faces whenever Uncle Laz cooked up one of his specialty pizzas at Parma Johns. I'd never—repeat, never—swooned over the smell of books. Nor could I imagine it.

"Bella, let's go to the Renaissance Literature section. There's a wonderful table there, just perfect to sit and discuss our wedding plans." Elizabeth practically skipped ahead of us.

Walter was distracted with his cell phone. Looked like the guy was answering an email. I understood the work ethic, but...really? Couldn't he give one hour to his bride-to-be for wedding prep?

I subtracted another ten points, bringing his overall husband-to-be scored down to a dismal fifty.

I followed on Elizabeth's heels to the table in question, my gaze traveling up, up, up at the bookshelves, filled with books of every sort. As I looked at them, I couldn't help but think of all those authors—each slaving away through the night, type, type, typing his or her manuscript to make it perfect for publication. In that moment I had a new appreciation for book-folks.

Well, sort of.

I watched from a distance as Walter shoved his phone into his back pocket then I offered a faint smile. "Glad you could join us, Bella."

I added ten points.

Then subtracted them again when he didn't pull out Elizabeth's chair before he plopped down into a seat. Ugh.

She sat next to him, clearly oblivious to the math equations going on in my head, and I took the chair across from them. I pulled my laptop out of my bag and set it on the gorgeous wood table.

Across from me, Elizabeth pulled out a tablet. "I'm loaded with ideas," she said. "They're all written down."

"That's my little OCD girl." Walter patted her hand. "If it's not in writing it doesn't count."

I subtracted another ten points. Only, by now I was having trouble keeping up with his score. If this kept up, I'd have to pull out a calculator.

"Walter thinks I'm OCD, but I'm really just organized." She giggled, my first clue that his words hadn't offended her. "I *love* being organized."

"Me too. I'm a firm believer in writing everything down," I concurred. "Makes it more real."

"Sure does."

My thoughts shifted back to the thousands of books surrounding me. Surely the writers felt exactly the same way. Having their stories—their words—written down had surely made their dreams more tangible.

Elizabeth turned on her tablet and we went to work on the wedding plans. Several times during our meeting Walter checked his email.

"Sorry, ladies," he said on about the fifth interruption, "but I've got some things stirring with my publisher. Big stuff." His eyebrows arched.

Elizabeth gave him a doe-eyed look as she placed her hand on his. "So proud of you, baby."

"Thanks, Lizzy." He gave her a little wink. *Ten points!*

Then took a phone call. *Negative ten points.*

Oh well. We'd just keep working without him.

Elizabeth and I went over the plans we'd already agreed upon: a book-themed wedding in the chapel at Club Wed, featuring some of her favorite female professors and friends as bridesmaids.

"You should see their dresses, Bella. Gorgeous fall colors. A beautiful mix."

"Sounds perfect. I told D.J. all about your color scheme and he's already working on the faux bookshelves for the reception hall. Have you figured out the centerpieces yet?"

"I have." Elizabeth scrolled around on her tablet until she located a couple of photos of flower arrangements and stacks of books, all worked together into gorgeous centerpieces.

As she showed me the beautiful pictures of fall-colored flowers, I couldn't help but gasp. "Wow."

"Right? I'd like to incorporate some autumn colors into the library theme. I think the reds, golds and browns will lend themselves nicely to the bookish feel, don't you?"

"Sure. Sounds good. Have you ordered everything?"

"Yes. I met with Cassia, the florist, just this morning. She recommended Asiatic lilies, Viking spray chrysanthemums, deep red roses, and a pretty mix of gerbera in orange and yellow. Oh, and oak leaves to trim it all out. What do you think?"

"I think we need a hayride and some pumpkins and we'll all be in a fall frame of mind." A little chuckle followed.

Still, gauging from the horrified expression the groom shot my way, I could tell he didn't find my words funny.

I subtracted ten more points.

Elizabeth, on the other hand, looked delighted. "Ooo, pumpkins. I'll have Cassia add a few of the little ones to the centerpieces. Thanks for the idea, Bella. They'll look good with all of the books I've picked out."

Walter must've panicked at this notion because he ended his call. Before long he started tossing in his two cents—okay, twenty cents—worth at every turn.

Still, we managed to solidify the plan: A lovely ceremony, featuring quotes from several of the classics in the text, and a library-themed reception, complete with D.J.'s bookish backdrop.

I could tell our meeting had come to its rightful end when Walter started responding to more emails.

"I think that's enough for today, Bella." Elizabeth turned off her tablet and pressed it into her oversized purse. "I've got you on speed-dial if I need anything. I—We can't thank you enough for all of your help."

"Yes, thank you, Bella." Walter offered me a warm smile.

I added ten points.

"Bella, before we leave, I'd like to show you something you're sure to appreciate." He rose and led the way to the psychology section of the library. Seconds later, he pointed out five books, all of which he'd written.

"Have you read these?" He glanced my way, looking like

a proud papa.

Should I tell him that the only books I'd read of late were the ones that I yawned through as I put my children to bed at night? And should I admit that I usually skipped pages to get to the end?

"I. . .I haven't." My confession sounded lame.

"Oh, you *should*." Elizabeth slipped her arm through Walter's. "He's absolutely brilliant, Bella. Lots of relationships have been saved, thanks to my guy."

The groom-to-be squared his shoulders.

"Let's check them all out so you can read them," he suggested.

And so, we did. Well, she did. Elizabeth used her library card to check out her fiance's books. He, of course, filled the ears of the librarian with tales of his fame as she stamped the books. She played along, even calling over a couple of her coworkers to ooh and aah over him. One of them recognized him from a local TV interview he'd done, and before long, Walter was signing bookmarks, which Elizabeth apparently carried in her purse for him.

While he rattled on about himself, I took one of his books in hand and flipped it over to read his bio on the back: The guy looked good in print. Maybe a little too good. I peered at him once more, trying to see him as these words had painted him— a true professional, compassionate, caring, kind.

Hmm.

As he left Elizabeth alone to carry her armload of books, I mentally subtracted another ten points. If this guy didn't shape up, before long we'd be working in negative numbers.

Chapter Two

FOR WHOM THE (WEDDING) BELL TOLLS

The second Tuesday in October I headed to Parma John's, my family's pizza restaurant. I always loved Tuesdays, because of the Pennies from Heaven special—my uncle's meatball pizza concoction. As I entered the restaurant, the sound of Dean Martin's voice greeted me. As he crooned the words to the familiar theme song: Every time it rains, it rains. . ." I whispered the words, "Pennies from Heaven."

"Hungry, eh?" Uncle Laz greeted me with a smile. "Should I toss one in the oven for you right now."

"She's already got one in the oven." The sound of my husband's voice rang out from behind me. I turned to see my handsome hunka-husband standing with his arms open wide. I gave him a hug.

"How's your day gone so far?" I asked him.

"Busier than a one-armed paper hanger, as my daddy used to say." He gave me a wink and pulled me close to press a kiss in my hair. "But better, now that I'm having a lunch date with my favorite gal."

"Aw, shucks." Did he know how to make a girl feel good, or what? That crazy psychologist-groom-fella could take some serious lessons from my husband.

D.J. walked me to a nearby table and pulled out a chair for me.

Ten points.

No, twenty points, because he gave me the sweetest smile I'd ever seen as he settled into place across from me.

"Back to the pizza. . ." Uncle Laz's voice rang out. "Medium or Large?"

"Extra large," I responded. "Expecting company. Incoming bride and groom."

"Should I be nervous?" Laz put his hands on his hips. Half the folks you do business with scare the britches off of me."

"The bride is nice." I gave him a strained smile.

Laz walked back toward the kitchen, muttering something that I couldn't quite make out. "Special, extra large!" he called out to my brother Nick, who worked in the kitchen.

"What's up with the groom?" D.J. asked. "Better tell me before they get here. I don't need any surprises."

So, I filled him in. He listened in silence, but shook his head several times as I spoke. "So, let me get this straight." D.J. looked perplexed. "He's a psychologist or whatever you call it."

"Yep."

"Only, no one can stand him."

"Well, his bride-to-be can stand him. She adores him. And from what I understand, folks in his field appreciate him. He has quite a few adoring fans among the women, too."

"Well, that makes me feel better." He rolled his eyes.

The bell at the door jingled and I looked up to discover my mother had entered, along with my Aunt Rosa. They made a beeline for us and sat down. Should I tell them I was expecting guests? Hmm. Judging from the look of consternation on my mother's face, maybe not.

"Bella, I have a bone to pick with you." My mother frowned.

"What, Mama?"

"I know you had an ultrasound last Friday. Sophia told me. I just don't understand why you won't tell us the sex of the baby."

"If you're wanting to keep it a secret, we won't tell anyone." Rosa gave me a hopeful look. "Promise."

"Humph." I knew better than that, of course.

"You guys don't understand." I shook my head as I looked back and forth between them. "We don't know the baby's sex. We don't want to know until he—or she—joins us in person in February. This will be our final little Neeley and we all want to be surprised."

Mama sighed. "I understand, but I want to start shopping, Bella. And how can we throw you a shower if we don't know the sex of the baby?" My mother's penetrating gaze caught me off-guard.

"A shower? For baby number five?"

"Sure, why not? We love to throw parties."

I put my hand up. "Folks, listen. . .I have more baby items than should be allowed by law. I've got cribs, strollers, bibs, bottles, clothes and diapers a'plenty. I've still got stuff left over from the shower you guys threw for the twins." When my mother's lips curled down in a pout, I reached over and gave her a hug. "Trust me, I appreciate the thought. But this time it's just not necessary. And if you feel the need to go on a shopping spree for this little one, wait until after he's born."

"He. You said he." Mama's eyes lit up. "It's a boy!"

"That was just the proverbial he. I truly don't know, and won't until the day of. So, bear with me."

The grumbling coming from Mama sounded a bit like a bear. An angry bear. Still, this was our decision, mine and D.J.'s, and we'd already made it.

"I don't understand why you still feel compelled to work, Bella." Mama gave me one of those motherly looks she'd become famous for. "Your sister is happy to help out at the wedding facility. And things are slowing down. It's fall."

"I'm just five months along, Mama. It's not like this baby's going to come any second now."

"I know, but the twins were early." The concern in her eyes alarmed me.

"This is different. The doctor isn't worried, so why should I be?"

"It's my job to worry, Bella. That's why God put me on this earth."

"He put you here to worry?" I shook my head. "Well, he should start paying you overtime, Mama, because you're extra-good at your job."

"Oh, thank you, honey. But I still think you should put your feet up." She mumbled the words, "For the next twenty years or so, until the kids are grown."

I glanced toward the door and Mama must've picked up on my anxiety. "You waiting on someone, Bella?"

"Yeah, incoming bride and groom in just a few minutes. Not sure you want to stick around for this one." I felt my nose wrinkle as I spoke the words.

"Say no more." Aunt Rosa shot up out of her chair. Well, as fast as an elderly woman with thirty extra pounds on her could shoot. "I just came down to talk to Laz about our next gig on The Food Network."

I couldn't help but smile as she and Mama made their way back to the kitchen. Who else had relatives with their own

18

program on The Food Network, after all?

Then again, who else had a family like mine? They might be loud. They might be crazy. But they were my people and I adored them.

"Do we have a couple of minutes before they get here?" D.J.'s voice startled me back to attention. "I'd like to go over what I've done so far."

"Yeah. About seven minutes, to be precise. And this bride is very, very precise."

"Ugh."

D.J. pulled out his phone and showed me some pictures of the work he'd started on the faux bookshelves for the upcoming reception. About six minutes into his explanation, Elizabeth and Walter showed up. I made introductions and they joined us at the table. Everyone looked to be in a good frame of mind, so I breathed a sigh of relief.

Well, until D.J. started showing them pictures of his work.

"So, here's the plan." My honey pointed to a picture on his phone. "I'm using Styrofoam to create faux bookshelves. They won't be very deep, just a few inches. But from a distance they'll look just like the real deal."

Walter's phone dinged and he pulled it out to read an incoming message. Ugh. Not again.

D.J., oblivious, flipped through a couple more pictures. Elizabeth *oohed* and *aahed* as she took in the life-sized faux bookshelves. Though they hadn't been painted yet, the beautiful pieces looked amazing.

Walter stopped texting and looked up, creases forming between his brows. "Styrofoam?" Walter glanced D.J.'s way with an "I'm not convinced" expression on his face.

"Stick with me here. It's not the kind like you use in coffee cups. This stuff is designed for set construction." D.J. lit into a lengthy conversation about the uses of styrofoam in theater productions. "Anyway, I'll paint them to look like bookshelves and will get Bella's mama to paint the books. She's quite the artist."

"All those years at the Opera House, helping with set construction," I explained. "She's great."

"Ooo, speaking of lovely things. . ." Elizabeth's eyes lit up. "The invitations were sent a couple of weeks back, Bella. Did you get yours? I sent you one just so you could see our colors."

"I did. I have to admit, I'd never seen anything like it before. Very clever. And definitely the right thing to put the guests in the mood for your book theme."

"Right?" She patted her groom-to-be's hand. "The library card style was Walter's idea, and I absolutely fell in love with it. You wouldn't believe how hard we had to search for a graphic designer to get it right, but we were thrilled with the outcome. Weren't we, Walter?"

"Yes, we—" His phone dinged again.

Elizabeth seemed oblivious. "You should see the programs. They match the invitations. Oh, and I ordered the cake a few days ago. Did Scarlet tell you?" Elizabeth glanced toward the opening to my sister-in-law's bakery. "It's going to be amazing."

"Scarlet never disappoints." I didn't have to work hard to sing my sister-in-law's praises. She was the very best in the cake biz.

"I just can't wait to tell you about the wedding cake." Elizabeth reached into her bag for her tablet. Seconds later her fingers went crazy on the keys and she came up with several online cake photos. "I've already showed Scarlet my sketches and she's onboard."

"Awesome." My gaze landed on the sketch of the most over-the-top cake I'd ever seen in my life. It looked like a library had opened up and hurled all over a cake.

Oh boy.

Yes, Scarlet was the best, but could she really pull off... this?

"What do you think?" Elizabeth released a little sigh as she pointed at her library-themed cake. "I just think it's dreamy. All of the books on the bottom tier really set the tone. And the second tier is a combination of some of the classics: If you look close, you'll see images from *Wuthering Heights*, *Pride and Prejudice*, and even *Little Women*. And the top tier? Isn't it perfect? It's a nod to Walter's latest book, *I'm Okay, You Need Some Work*."

Walter squared his shoulders and shoved his phone aside.

"I asked Scarlet to make the whole thing kind of wonky, so it has an *Alice in Wonderland* feel."

"I.. .I see that."

Walter grunted as he looked at the sketch.

"What, honey?" She glanced his way.

"*Alice in Wonderland*? For a wedding cake?"

"Well, don't you get it? Every single aspect of the reception will be something literary, not just the cake. But it has to fit in. *Alice in Wonderland* for the cake. Raspberry cordial from *Anne of Green Gables* for the punch. Clam chowder from *Moby Dick*. Turkish Delight from *The Chronicles of Narnia*. Bubble and Squeak from *The Wind in the Willows*.

"Bubble and Squeak?" For the first time in what felt like ages my husband piped up. God bless him. He'd kept quiet during the cake conversation.

"Turkish Delight?" Walter slapped himself on the

forehead. "What is this, a children's play or a wedding?"

"But. . .but. . .I thought you were onboard for a literary-themed reception." Elizabeth's lower lip curled down in a pout. "Oh, Walter, I had no idea you would be disappointed."

"Literary, yes. But can't we come up with something other than children's stories."

"I mentioned Moby Dick. And Wuthering Heights. And Pride and Prejudice."

"And *Little Women*," D.J. threw in.

"All aimed at females." Walter signed and leaned back in his chair. Frankly, I didn't blame him this time. I might just have to give the boy some bonus points for not flipping out.

Elizabeth gave him a pensive look. "Remember that scene in *A Tale of Two Cities* where Sydney performs the ultimate act of love by laying down his life for Charles?"

The groom-to-be paled. "You're asking me to die in your place?"

"No, Walter." Elizabeth shook her head and then muttered, "Not literally, anyway," under her breath. "I'm just saying that we need to be willing to give a little. That's all."

This led to the oddest conversation I'd ever witnessed from the groom. He lit into some sort of psycho-babble that went over my head. D.J. excused himself to go to the men's room. Coward.

On and on Walter went, talking about things that seemed completely foreign to me.

When he finally came up for air, Elizabeth piped up. "Walter, remember the theme of *Robinson Crusoe*? The unlikely leader called out of his comfort zone?"

"I thought he was shipwrecked."

"Point is, he was called upon to do something unsettling. That's all I'm asking, Walter."

"You want me to crash my boat onto a private island?"

Elizabeth's head dropped into her hands and she mumbled, "Only on some days."

Oh boy.

Oh boy, oh boy.

Chapter Three

A WRINKLE IN TIME

We somehow made it through the rest of the conversation without anyone losing it. Uncle Laz lifted the mood when he delivered the meatball pizza to the table. Walter's eyes lit up as he grabbed his first slice. A few minutes later, D.J. excused himself to head back to work. I rose and followed him to the door, where I gave him a grateful kiss.

"You've got your hands full with these folks, Bella." D.J. whispered in my ear. "Want to put out an S.O.S.? I'm sure Sophia would take over for you."

"Nah. I'll be okay." A little pause followed on my end. "Can I ask you a question, though?"

"Shore," he drawled.

"You heard what Mama said earlier. She thinks I need to quit my job. Do you agree with that?"

He shrugged. "I thought things were slowing down."

"They are. I've just got a couple of weddings this fall and another one in January. Totally manageable. But she's got this idea that I'm ready for a full-time transition into home life, that I should give up completely on wedding planning."

"The feminists haven't gotten to her yet, eh?" He quirked

a brow.

"Never!" I laughed. "Have you met my mama?"

"Yeah, I've met her. She spends half of her time caring for the family, the other half working at the Opera House. For free. Donating her time."

"Right. But she didn't start doing all of that until us kids were grown. You know? Maybe that's her beef. I don't think she understands that some women work outside the home *and* raise a family. It seems like a foreign concept to her."

"You're overthinking this, Bella. Just pray about it. If the work is overwhelming. . ."

"It's not. I mean, it has been, in years past. But it's not right now."

"Pray about it. Just because someone gives advice doesn't mean you have to take it." He gave me a knowing look. "Only, now I'm going to give you some advice: run as fast and as far as you can from this bride and groom."

His boyish laughter caused me to roll my eyes. I watched as he disappeared out of the front door, then I turned around to head back to the table.

Only, my brother Nick sidled up next to me before I got a chance.

"Who are these people, Bella?" He narrowed his gaze as he took Walter and Elizabeth in. "Don't think I've seen them before."

Aunt Rosa and Mama stepped into place alongside Nick.

"Haven't seen the woman before, but that fella looks familiar." Rosa squinted.

After a few seconds, Mama clamped a hand over her mouth and her eyes widened. She pulled her hand down and whispered, "Oh. Boy."

"Right?" My palms instinctively went up. "That's all I can

say when he's around, too."

"Please tell me you're not swoonin' over his looks, Mama." Nick rolled his eyes. "That would just be creepy."

My mother pulled her hand down and shook her head. "No. Not swooning at all. Just taking it all in. This is the guy on that psycho-babble radio talk show. He's also been a frequent guest on Houston Today, that mid-day show on NBC."

Rosa snapped her fingers. "Yep. That's where I know him from."

"Who are we talking about?" Uncle Laz's voice sounded and I turned to see he was standing behind me holding some empty drink glasses. "That serious looking fellow with the phone addiction?"

"Yeah." I sighed.

"If you know what's good for you, you will not engage the man in conversation." I gave my uncle a knowing look.

"I know better than to ask his opinion about relationships." Mama shivered. "Listened to a few minutes of one of his programs and it was all I could take not to punch him through the air waves."

Uncle Laz set the empty drink cups down on a nearby table and wiped his palms on his apron. "I ain't afraid 'a no psycho-babble fella."

"He'll talk your ear off, that's all. Trust me when I say that you won't be able to get a word in edgewise."

Uncle Laz snorted. "Seriously? Since when hasn't your old uncle been able to get a word in edgewise? Watch a pro in action, Bella-bambina."

He grabbed a pitcher of soda from the counter and sauntered over to Elizabeth and Walter's table to greet them and refill their sodas. I watched as he engaged them in light conversation. At some point, their friendly chatter must've taken a terrifying turn. Uncle Laz glanced our way, panic in his eyes. Ten minutes later, he was seated at the table with the duo. Fifteen minutes after that, he looked our way, silently shouting, "Call 9-1-1" with his eyes.

"What do we do?" Rosa asked. "Stage an intervention?"

I glanced at the clock on the wall. "No. I have it on good authority Walter has to leave in fifteen minutes. At this point I'm giving the groom ten extra points for hanging around this long."

"Points?" Mama looked confused. I'd have to explain later.

By the time Laz rejoined us, I was worried about his health. The poor man had experience heart issues in the past, after all. Beads of sweat sat atop his furrowed brow. He tromped by us and muttered, "Don't. Say. A. Word."

I wouldn't dare. Poor guy.

Okay, time to head back to the table to say my goodbyes. I whispered a prayer for stamina and then headed that way. For whatever reason, Mama and Aunt Rosa decided to join me. I made introductions and they lit into easy chatter. Good. We needed a respite. Things went really well until Elizabeth showed Mama and Aunt Rosa the sketch of her wedding cake.

"Well, that's. . .different." Mama offered a strained smile.

"Told you, Elizabeth." Walter used his napkin to wipe some pizza sauce off of his chin. "That design isn't going to fly at a wedding."

"I have to agree with the groom, here." Aunt Rosa's nose wrinkled. "I used to make wedding cakes and this one looks more like something you'd see at a birthday party. Or maybe a book signing or something like that."

Oh boy.

Elizabeth gave Aunt Rosa a piercing gaze. "Perhaps you're familiar with O'Henry's classic tale, *The Gift of the Magi*."

"I, um. . .no." Rosa shook her head.

"It's the story of a woman who sold her hair clip to buy her husband a watch chain, only to find out that her husband sold his watch to buy her a beautiful hair clip, only to find out that she'd cut off all of her hair."

"That's the most pitiful thing I've ever heard." Mama fanned herself. "That whole problem could've been solved with one text message. Why didn't the wife just send a message to her husband before cutting off her hair?"

"I cut off my hair once," Rosa said. "Looked awful. That's why I kept it long. I can always pull it up into a knot when I'm cooking."

"I love your hair, sweetheart." Laz sauntered up and gave Rosa a kiss on the forehead. "Don't pay a bit of attention to that stupid story. Keep your hair."

"Point is, sometimes people make sacrifices for the greater good." Elizabeth gave Walter a stern look.

He decided this would be a terrific time to head back to work. I couldn't exactly blame the guy. Psychologist or not, he couldn't seem to find the right words to pacify this anxious bride-to-be.

Hopefully I would figure out how to maneuver this ship into port. Until then. . .

All of this adding and subtracting was about to drive me nuts.

Chapter Four

PRIDE AND PREJUDICE

A couple of days after our infamous meeting at Parma Johns, I'd settled back into my work. D.J. stopped by the wedding facility mid-afternoon on Thursday, just before picking up the older kids from school. As he settled into a chair in my office I couldn't help but notice he looked nervous, like he had something on his mind.

"Okay, spill the beans." I gave him an "Out with it" look.

"Who, me?"

"Yeah, you. You're up to something."

He squirmed in his chair and his gaze shifted to the clock. "It's just, well. . .I'm thinking ahead to Christmas, honey."

"Christmas?" I groaned and then closed my laptop. "Don't remind me. I haven't started shopping yet."

"You have plenty of time. But I'm thinking of a gift that's a little different from the usual."

"What kind of gift?"

He grabbed his phone and went straight to his Internet browser. "Now, don't kill me, Bella."

"Um, okay."

"Would it be okay to ask for forgiveness in advance?" His

eyes met mine.

"Um, sure, but what does this have to do with Christmas?"

"I might have already planned a little gift for the kids."

"Why would that bother me?"

He opened an email and then turned the phone my way. I gasped when I saw a picture of a large golden retriever. "W-what am I looking at?"

"Her name is Goldie. She's pregnant."

"Congratulations?" I offered.

"She belongs to one of my construction guys. Her puppies are due just before Halloween. You know what this means, right?" His gaze shifted back down to the photo on his phone.

"That your friend won't be trick or treating with his kids that night?" I tried.

"He's a single guy, Bella. No kids." D.J. enlarged the picture and his smile broadened. "Isn't she a beauty?"

"D.J. No. We just lost Precious a few weeks ago."

He gave me a pleading look. "Think about it, Bella. Goldie's puppies will be eight weeks old, come Christmas. I was thinking about getting a little boy, one with a lot of spunk, but great with the kids."

"D.J. I don't know if we're ready for another dog. Not yet."

"I'm not trying to replace Precious, Bella. I'm not. I just think the kids are ready. And I'll feel better with a dog in the house to protect us, especially if we're really talking about moving to a bigger place with more yard space."

I sighed. A new baby meant an eventual change in living arrangements. Were we really talking about moving? Now?

Just about the time I was ready to say, "Go ahead and get the dog," the phone rang. D.J. scooted out of the office to pick up the kids, the words, "Pray about it, Bella," his last thoughts on the matter.

I took the call, my thoughts firmly planted on the dog situation and my husband's heartbreaking expression as he'd talked about how the kids needed a new canine companion.

The sobbing on the other end of the phone caught me completely off-guard.

"B-Bella?"

Elizabeth. I could barely make out her next few words through the sniffles, though.

"Oh, Bella, the most awful thing has happened."

My heart skipped a beat. When brides started a conversation with those words, things usually didn't end well.

"What is it, Elizabeth?" I shifted the phone to my other ear.

"It's Walter."

Ack. Had he left her, unable to deal with the *Alice in Wonderland* wedding cake? Or, worse yet, had he. . .No, I wouldn't think like that.

She began to ramble, but I couldn't make sense of it.

"This whole thing is just a mess!" she wailed.

"Wait. *What* whole thing? I thought we had all of our ducks in a row."

"We did, but then ThinkThrough Publishing Company got out a shotgun and went to town, killing them."

"Elizabeth, you're going to have to start at the beginning. Not sure I'm getting this." I knew there were dead ducks involved, but other than that, I couldn't make a lick of sense out of the girl's emotional tirade.

"Bella, they're sending him on a book tour. ThinkThrough just informed him that they've set up a tour for *I'm Okay, You Need Work.*"

"Wait, what? Do they realize he's in the middle of

wedding plans?"

"His publicist says he should be able to do both, but... seriously? It's a six-state tour, with multiple cities in each state. And he's got to somehow keep his practice going, too. I have no idea how he's going to do it. He's already so. . .so. . ." She sighed. "Anyway, he's already very distracted. We'll just leave it at that. But now? He's going to be gone, I'm going to implement our plans by myself, and he'll hate them. Just like he hated the cake."

"I'll be here to help you, Elizabeth. And we can include him in the conversations with Facetime or Skype. Right?"

"I guess." She sniffled. "It's just not going to be the same. Trust me when I say that he's the sort to take a vested interest, so I have to get this right. If I don't, he'll make me change it at the last minute."

Hmm. That knocked another ten points off of the man's already diminishing score.

On and on she went, pouring out her heart. After a moment, Elizabeth's voice cracked. "Oh, B-Bella! I can't believe I'm so emotional. Please don't tell Walter, okay?"

I wanted to say, "Why would it matter to your fiancé if you got emotional?" but didn't. I had no idea how his thought processes worked in these situations.

"He always tells me just to breathe. But I am breathing, you know? I mean, I'd be dead otherwise, right? And I'm clearly not dead, though—and please don't tell him this part, either—I wish I was."

"Dead?" My heart skipped a beat.

"Well, not really, but you know what I mean. I wish I was. His new book has taken off. I think we have you to blame for that, to be honest."

"Me?"

"Yes. You didn't notice the endorsement your Uncle Laz gave on the radio show yesterday afternoon?"

"Uncle Laz was on Walter's radio show?"

"He called in to ask a question about marriage, and before long Walter had converted him to his way of thinking. He does that, you know."

"Does what?"

"Converts people. Wins them over. And that's what he's trying to do now, Bella. He's trying to win me over to his way of thinking that it won't matter if he's gone while we're planning the wedding."

"Elizabeth, remember what you said earlier: the planning part is done. It's up to the vendors now to follow through and do their thing. You just have to trust them."

"You. Don't. Know. Walter." She sniffled. "He'll be calling me every day to check on this little thing or that little thing. I'll be drowning in a sea of details by the time he gets home."

I glanced at the clock. By now, D.J. was probably pulling up to the school to fetch Tres and little Rosie. I needed to go next door and pick up the twins, then head home to meet them.

"Elizabeth, I have an idea. When does Walter leave?"

"In a week." She blew her nose.

"Great. What are you doing this Saturday? Can you come down to the island?"

"I. . .I think that will work. Why?"

"We're having a big fall festival at my parents' church—the big Methodist one on Broadway. The whole family will be there. Bring Walter down and we'll pow-wow. We'll knock out the final plans and then you'll have less to stress about once he's gone."

She sighed, and then her voice seemed to brighten. "A

33

festival sounds really fun, Bella. Kind of like that scene in *Little Women* where Jo and Meg celebrate May Day around the maypole."

I had no idea what she meant by that, but apparently she liked the idea.

I gave her the details of the festival and she promised to meet me at 10:00 A.M. As we ended the call, I gave the clock one last glance. If I left right now, I could get the twins and be home in time to greet my husband and children.

As I rose, a little fluttering in my belly caught me off-guard. I put my hand on my tummy and grinned. "Yes, little one, I know. Mommy's been very busy and hasn't had as much time to think about all of the changes you will bring to our world."

Like, a new house.

And more chaos.

And. . .a dog?

Chapter Five

ALL QUIET ON THE WESTERN FRONT

Saturday dawned with an unexpected heat wave. Temperatures soared into the early 90s, which had everyone on edge, particularly those of us who had agreed to help set up for the event.

Well, I wasn't exactly hauling things around, not in my condition, but I watched as D.J. and his brother, Bubba, did. Uncle Laz seemed put off by the whole thing. I had a feeling he was more irritated at the fact that this was a Methodist event than anything. He and Aunt Rosa attended St. Patrick's, the Catholic church down the street.

He grumbled all morning long.

Me? I adored every second of watching things come together—the petting zoo, which I knew my children would love. The pony rides, sure to be a big hit with little Rosie. The rock climbing wall, which Tres would flip over. Well, not *literally* flip. I hoped.

And the cake walk? Even the little ones would enjoy that. We would all have a blast at the photo booth area, not to mention the dozens of game booths, complete with candy prizes. By the time this day ended, we'd be sugared up and exhausted. But for now, Mama—who'd agreed to oversee the day's events—was scurrying to and fro, making sure everything was ready to go.

By the time everything was in place, the first guests were arriving. Time to get my kiddos into their costumes. Tres had decided to come as Spiderman. Rosie, of course, had opted for Cinderella. My favorite? The twins. I'd dressed my little ones as Elsa and Anna from the movie, *Frozen*.

The festivities got underway in short order. D.J.'s parents arrived. I gave my mother-in-law, Earline, a hug.

"You look radiant, Bella," she said. "Now, tell me what that ultrasound tech said. Are we having a boy baby or a girl?"

"Mama Neeley, we told you, we're not going to find out until the baby comes."

Tiny creases appeared between her eyes. "Well, I know you said that, but I didn't really think you meant it."

"We meant it, Mama." D.J. gave her a stern look. "And I've told you that at east three times, including on the phone yesterday."

Earline sighed. "A woman can try, can't she?"

She could try, all right, but that wouldn't get her anywhere.

"I think y'all should move up to Splendora," D.J.," his father said. "We've got plenty of land. C'mon up and build yourself a nice big house. Raise those kids in the country like you were raised."

Oh boy.

Time to change the direction of this conversation.

"Ready to go to have some fun?" I called out, my voice as cheerful as possible.

After a bit of conversation D.J. and I split up—he and his parents took the older two children to several booths geared toward their age group and I took the twins to the toddler area. Though we had a wonderful time, I couldn't stop sweating. Ugh. Why hadn't I worn a short-sleeved shirt?

Just as we headed to the picnic area around noon, a familiar voice rang out. "Bella! Yoo-hoo!"

I turned to see three of my favorite people—Twila, Jolene and Bonnie Sue. I had to laugh when the trio took steps toward me in their over-the-top nursery rhyme attire. Twila had come as Little Bo Peep. Wow. Jolene? If I had to guess, I'd say she was the Old Woman Who Lived in a Shoe. And Bonnie Sue? Well, I'd never seen anyone dressed as a teapot before, but there was a first time for everything, right?

They drew near, creating quite a stir among my family members, who oohed and aahed over the lavish costumes. The women seemed to relish in the attention.

Well, all but Jolene. "Ugh. Why did I wear this long-sleeved shirt?" She groaned and tugged at her collar. "It's so hot out here, I could melt into the pavement."

"If it's any consolation, you look divine." Mama reached out to finger the ruffles on her blouse. "I haven't see anything this sweet since Rosa used to smock Bella and Sophia's dresses."

"Thank you." Jolene stopped fidgeting with her attire. She pulled out a battery propelled misting fan and pointed it toward her face. "Though, I can't help but wonder if the Lord forgot to flip the page on his calendar. Feels like September weather, not mid-October."

This led to a lengthy discussion about the weather. By now, D.J. had joined us and the kids were getting restless. I agreed to let them have popcorn balls. I'd probably regret it later, but today was all about celebration.

As the kids nibbled on their treats, Twila slipped her arm

over my shoulder. "Bella, honey, I heard about your sweet puppy."

I felt the sting of tears in my eyes at once.

"Precious lived a good, long life." I spoke over the lump in my throat. "I guess it was just her time." I gave her a little shrug. "It's been a few weeks now, but D.J.'s really struggling. I think he took it harder than I did, if you want the truth of it."

"He's a country boy, honey," she said with a knowing smile. "Country boys love their dogs. They can't live without 'em."

Okay, now I had to wonder if D.J. had put her up to this. Did she know about the golden retriever puppies?

Before I could give this another thought, she headed off to the photo booth with the other ladies. Aunt Rosa offered to take my kiddos to the photo booth, as well, to have their pictures made. I'd just started to join them when Elizabeth and Walter arrived. D.J. took the opportunity to scurry off to the photo booth with the kids. Great.

I'd forgotten to warn my guests that this was a costumed event, but they didn't seem terribly put off by it. Well, until Walter caught a glimpse of Bonnie Sue in her teacup outfit, off in the distance.

"What have we here?" he asked. "A theatrical?"

Should I tell him that everything about the Splendora ladies was theatrical?

Elizabeth's face lit up. "Ooo, costumes! If I'd known, I would've come as Jo from *Little Women*. She's my very favorite."

"I would've come as. . ." Walter paused. "Me."

I subtracted ten points.

The two of them headed over to the food vendors to buy some lunch. In the meantime, Twila, Bonnie Sue and Jolene bounded my way.

Jolene stared after the bride and groom-to-be, her cheeks as red as the ruby lipstick she'd chosen to wear today. "Bella, why didn't you tell us?"

"Tell you what?"

"That's. . .That's. . ." She pointed at Walter, her mouth agape.

Twila grunted. "Jolene, close your mouth. It's not a garage door."

Jolene closed her mouth. Then opened it again to speak. "I know that man. He's. . .he's. . ."

Either the heat had done a number on her, or she was too mesmerized by Walter to continue.

Twila rolled her eyes. "Honestly, I don't know what's come over you. You're a married woman, after all."

"I. . .I know." Jolene fanned herself. "But that's Walter Yargo. I listen to his talk show every week. Can't get enough of his latest book, *I'm Okay, You Need Some Work*. I bought a copy for my husband."

Twila snorted.

"I just think he's amazing." Jolene sighed in a fan-girl sort of way. "You know?" She gave me an imploring look.

I didn't know. I still couldn't figure out why so many folks found this guy so admirable when I could barely tolerate him.

A few minutes later the bride and groom-to-be returned with their food. I introduced them to the Splendora trio, and Elizabeth gushed over their costumes.

"You'll never know how tickled I am to see you choosing literary costumes," she said as she clasped her hands together. "Rarely do you see people dress up as characters from stories or books. Movies, sure? But, books?"

Okay, I suddenly hoped she wouldn't see my children's costumes.

Nah, it didn't matter what anyone thought. They looked adorable.

Bonnie Sue continued to tug at the collar of her blouse, whining about the heat.

"Oh, I know." Elizabeth concurred. "I can't stand it." She paused and a dreamy look came over her. "Do you ever wish you lived in New England, or someplace where the changing of the leaves would make you feel like autumn had really come?"

"What? And miss these lovely temperatures in the upper 80s?" Twila snorted.

"There's nothing like New England in the fall," Elizabeth crooned. "Have you read *Walden*, by Henry David Thoreau?"

"No, but I knew a fella named Henry." Bonnie Sue wrinkled her nose. "Broke my heart in sixth grade. I heard he ended up going to jail for tax evasion."

Walter rolled his eyes.

"Another great classic set in New England is Nathaniel Hawthorne's amazing story, *The Scarlet Letter*." Elizabeth patted Bonnie Sue's arm. "Surely you've read that one. It's required reading in high school."

"Haven't been to high school in years," Bonnie Sue responded. "But I do know a gal named Scarlet. Runs the local bakery."

"*The Scarlet Letter* is one of my favorites," Walter said. "It presents the reader with an in-depth look into the soul of mankind and the role that hidden guilt and shame play on the human psyche."

"We don't believe in psychics, honey," Bonnie Sue said with the wave of a hand. "We're Full Gospel."

This took the conversation in a completely different direction. Before long this boisterous group was hot and heavy into chatter about denominations. I found myself looking for my husband and children. Could I escape the inevitable and just spend a little time with my family?

From the looks of things. . .no.

"Did you guys hear that Bubba's playing Jean ValJean in *Les Miserables* at the Opera House?" Twila asked, after they'd played out the Full Gospel conversation.

"No." I gasped. "Oh, that's my favorite."

"Mine too." Twila's eyes fluttered closed. "Oh, I love that scene where Valjean steals the silver from the convent—at least, I think it was a convent. Right?—but then the priest forgives him. Isn't that just the most wonderful expression of grace ever?"

Elizabeth reached over to squeeze Twila's hand and her eyes misted over. "I. Cry. Every. Time."

"Me. Too!" Twila swiped at her eyes with the back of her hand.

"Can you even imagine forgiving someone who stole your most valuable possession?" Jolene asked.

"One time Wanda Kay Collier tried to steal my boyfriend." Bonnie Sue's eyes narrowed. "Happened back in high school. Ain't no woman ever gonna steal a fella from me and live to tell about it."

Walter coughed.

I added ten points to his score for putting up with these ladies.

"Bonnie Sue, for pity's sake. I've heard that story a hundred times and it grows bigger every time I hear it." Twila slapped herself on the forehead. "If you recall, *you* tried to steal that fella away from Wanda, not the other way around."

41

"Well, it doesn't change the point of my story." Bonnie Sue rolled her eyes. "I can't abide a thief."

"I thought we were talking about forgiveness." Elizabeth looked perplexed. "Right?"

"Oh, I've forgiven Wanda Kay, because that's the kind of Christian I am." Bonnie Sue squared her shoulders. "I do as the Bible says."

"Except when she's stealin' another woman's fella," Jolene whispered in my ear.

I snorted.

"There've been plenty of times I've had to forgive folks for hurting my feelings," Jolene added. "When I first started teasin' my hair, nearly half a dozen folks in Splendora made fun of me. They told me I was stuck in the 60s." They didn't know I was teasing my hair 'cause my scalp was showin' through. I mean, it's one thing for a woman's slip to show, but for her scalp to show?" Jolene shivered. "I couldn't bear it. So, I started teasing it up and now no one notices."

"Except for that one little patch in back," Twila said. "But it's hardly noticeable when you brush your hair sideways like that."

This somehow led to a conversation about Donald Trump's hair.

Which somehow led to a conversation about the current political climate.

Which somehow led to a conversation about the state of our country.

At this point, my mother-in-law joined us again. Earline Neeley was extremely passionate about her presidential candidate of choice, so she filled our ears with her thoughts on the matter.

Oh boy.

All the while, Walter remained painfully quiet.

I added ten points so many times I lost count.

"I thought we were talking about forgiveness," I said, in an attempt to get this train back on track. "Or am I just suffering from A.D.D.?"

"Oh, I forgave those folks for ridiculing my lily white scalp," Jolene said.

"But your A.D.D. comment reminds me of a time when folks in Splendora accused me of being OCD." Twila grimaced. "Just because I color-coordinate my closet."

"And check the locks on your front door seven times before you leave," Jolene added.

"And then go back inside your house to make sure you didn't leave the stove on," Bonnie Sue threw in.

Twila's eyes narrowed to slits. "I did leave the stove on once, silly, which is why I feel compelled to go back inside to check. And I'm not really all that bad. I only check the locks six times, not seven."

Jolene rolled her eyes.

"Point is, I always forgive folks for hurting my feelings." Twila glared at Jolene. "Even when they overstep their bounds."

Jolene gave her a knowing look. "You didn't forgive Mayor Deets when he gave you a run for your money during the election."

"I not only forgave him, I made the peace. And I won that election fair and square, I'll have you know."

"Never said you didn't." Jolene put her hands on her ample hips.

"But *I* took the real prize." Bonnie Sue clasped her hands together. "I married Tommy Deets!"

At this point, Walter decided to get involved. Apparently

his psychology background included units on both A.D.D. and O.C.D., which he felt would be helpful to the ladies.

Not that they paid him a bit of attention. No, by now they'd gotten distracted with the cotton candy vendor on the other side of the field. Just about the time Walter wrapped up his lengthy lecture on A.D.D., Jolene took off, chasing the pink fluffy confection. The other ladies followed on her heels.

I sighed as I turned to face the bride and groom-to-be. "Welcome to my world."

Elizabeth placed her hand on my arm. "I *love* your world, Bella. It's colorful and bright and loaded with characters nearly as fun as many I've studied in my books."

"Oh, they're characters, all right." And, as I stared at the trio of ladies with cotton candy in their hands, I had to admit they would be perfect for the literary stage.

If only I could find the time to pen their story, I might just become a millionaire.

Chapter Six

WAR AND PEACE

I didn't really get a chance to talk with Elizabeth and Walter about the wedding, what with the festivalgoers offering so many interruptions. So, I invited them back to my parents' home to hang out with our family when I felt we'd had enough fun.

My sister stayed behind with all of the kids, who were begging for more time at the festival. I didn't blame them. Poor little darlings. Their mama was too preoccupied with grownups to show them a good time. Shame on me.

Of course, they loved staying with Sophia and her husband, and all the more when she offered to take the kids back to our place after the festival so that they could be bathed and put down for bed. I would miss my babies, but the idea of having some peace and quiet this evening sounded divine.

D.J. drove me back to my parents' place. I noticed the concern on his face. "Bella," he said after a period of silence, "I hope you don't mind if I state the obvious, but I'm not sure you're going to get much done with Elizabeth and Walter, especially with my parents coming to your parents' place for dinner. You know my dad. He's liable to say something to set

Walter off."

"Walter's a psychologist, D.J. He'll handle it fine, I'm sure. I have to at least try to get Elizabeth calmed down before Walter leaves town tomorrow. She's my chief concern right now. And how bad could it be, really? They're good people. I'm sure the evening will go fine."

"Yeah. Hope so." He sighed, my first indication that D.J. was growing a little weary with all of this wedding-stuff. Hmm. Something to think about.

When we arrived at my parents' place, D.J. drove into the driveway and his parents pulled in behind us. Walter squealed his black Porsche to a halt behind them. I could tell the minute Walter and Elizabeth climbed out of his car that they had been squabbling. Her expression hid nothing. I plastered on a smile and did my best to look cheerful.

As soon as we made our way into the foyer of the spacious Victorian, Guido—our family parrot—started warbling out a song.

Elizabeth gasped and took several steps in his direction. "Oh, Bella! You have a parrot." For the first time in awhile, she smiled. Like, really, really smiled.

"Technically, Guido is my Uncle Laz's parrot," I explained. "But we've all adopted him."

"Oh, he's adorable." She went right up to his perch and stuck out her hand. "Hello there, little guy. How are you today?"

He released a shrill, "Go to the mattresses!"

"Oh, *The Godfather*!" Elizabeth clasped her hands together. "I taught a unit on that story last year. Fantastic takeaways! So many lessons to be learned."

"Like, don't let a horse in your bed," D.J.'s dad said, and then passed on through the foyer to the restroom.

"Lots of deep-rooted familial issues in that story," Walter said with a nod. "A little therapy could've turned that whole family around."

"Talking about us Rossis, eh?" Uncle Laz entered the foyer and slung his arm over Walter's shoulder. "I don't mind admitting it. We could all use some therapy."

"Oh, well, no. I was. . ." Walter couldn't seem to figure out what to say next. Funny, that my uncle could have that effect on a psychologist.

Laz gave him a winning smile. "Son, I have to tell you how much that book of yours is changing my life. It's working wonders on my marriage, too. Right, Rosa?"

She nodded as she passed by on her way to the kitchen. "Sure is. Just telling Earline about it now. Want to join me to get the food ready, honey?"

"Well, shore," Earline drawled. "Can't wait to hear more."

Really? Had Uncle Laz and Aunt Rosa lost their minds or was there something to this book after all?

I led the way into the living room while Guido called out "Go to the mattresses" a couple dozen more times. Lovely.

Rosa headed into the kitchen to start dinner, but returned a couple of minutes later with some snacks—a bowlful of mixed nuts and another bowl of mints.

"Don't eat too much, folks," she said. "We've got a yummy lasagna coming up. Made it before the festival. Just need to heat it up."

"Sounds wonderful." Walter's eyes sparkled with anticipation. "I can't tell you the last time I had a really good lasagna."

"I baked lasagna last weekend," Elizabeth said, and then sighed.

Walter kissed her on the cheek. "Well, other than that, I

mean."

Mama offered to help in the kitchen, but Rosa muttered something under her breath in response. These days, she didn't care much for Mama's help. My mother wasn't the best cook on the island. Still, she joined Rosa and Earline, if for no other reason than to escape our guests. I didn't blame her.

As Walter and Elizabeth settled onto the sofa, D.J., Pop and Laz took the recliners facing the large-screen TV. My father turned on the television. College football. Thank goodness. I hadn't really planned to include my relatives in the wedding planning, but maybe the game would distract them. D.J. looked content to avoid the bride and groom.

I sat next to Elizabeth on the sofa, ready to get to business. "Sorry things were so crazy at the festival. Guess that was kind of a wash. But we're here now. Let's wrap things up."

And that's exactly what we did. I went through a complete checklist of things for the wedding, covering everything from the wedding party to the vendors. I couldn't believe how quickly we got through everything. At some point along the way D.J.'s father slipped in the room. He found a spot on the ottoman and watched the game with the guys.

"See?" I offered Elizabeth a big smile when we wrapped up. "I told you we'd get through this before Walter had to leave town."

"Walter. Leave town." Her eyes immediately filled with tears.

"Oh no, not again." He leaned down and placed his face in his hands. "Please don't get worked up, Elizabeth."

"You always say I'm worked up, Walter. I'm just. . ." Her voice choked. "F-F-Female!"

This got the attention of every man in the room. D.J. looked my way, alarm in his eyes. His father quirked a brow then muttered something under his breath.

Walter lowered his voice and patted Elizabeth on the knee. "Honey, I'm trying to understand your feelings. You know that. It's what I do."

"Humph." A couple of tears dribbled over her lashes. "It's what you do for others, not me."

Okay, then.

D.J. excused himself to call Sophia to check on the children. His father decided he needed to tighten the screws in our front doorknob. Laz shot out of the room, claiming he needed to help Rosa in the kitchen. Only Pop remained, but he seemed glued to the game.

That left me to fend for myself. Should I stay or should I go?

Despite his training as a professional, Walter didn't seem to mind getting personal in front of the wedding planner. Weird.

Elizabeth swiped her eyes with the back of her hand. "Walter, you know that infamous scene in *The Last Leaf.*"

"Sure." He shrugged. "What about it?"

"Wait, the last *what*?" Pop asked.

"*The Last Leaf.*" Elizabeth seemed to lose herself in her ponderings for a moment. "One of the most beautiful classics ever written."

"I had a classic once," Pop chimed in. "A '68 Mustang. Red. Man, was she a beauty."

Elizabeth pinched her eyes shut and appeared to be counting to ten. When she popped them back open, she gave my father a strained smile. "I'm referring to a literary classic. *The Last Leaf* is the story of an artist who sacrifices his life by going out into the icy cold to paint a leaf on a wall so that a little girl can live."

"That's the dumbest thing I've ever heard of." Pop raked his fingers through his thinning hair. "Are you saying he died because he wanted to paint something?"

"Yes." Elizabeth nodded. "Well, sort of. The point is, he was willing to risk everything to give this little girl hope." She turned to face Walter. "And that's really all I'm asking for now, honey. Hope. I need to have hope that this is going to work out, that we're still going to pull off an amazing wedding, even though you're traveling across the United States instead of staying here in Texas, helping me."

"Elizabeth, really?" Walter crossed his arms at his chest. "I'm only going to six states, and we're just talking a couple of weeks. You're an amazing, brilliant woman. You can pull this off without me."

Ten points!

"Point is, I don't want to do it without you."

Something rather strange happened at this point. Walter slipped into psycho-babble again. He began to speak to her in much the same way a doctor would speak to a patient. Granted, about half of what he said went over my head, but I managed to get the gist of it. He wanted her to get ahold of her emotions.

Oh boy.

I got my first clue that she didn't plan to cooperate when her face turned red. Elizabeth stared her groom-to-be down. "You're so incredibly prideful, Walter."

"I am not." He squared his shoulders and puffed out his chest. "I'm just confident, that's all. I know my stuff, and I don't mind sharing what I know. There's a distinct difference between pride and confidence."

"There's no difference, not in your case, anyway. You're prideful. Just like Mr. Darcy."

"Wait." My father glanced my way and muttered, "Who's Mr. Darcy? Is this gal seeing someone else?"

"No, Pop." I gave him a warning look to keep quiet. "He's a character in a novel."

"Oh, I try never to read novels." My father reached for the TV remote. "Hard on my eyes. Give me a good action flick any day. Or a game."

He turned up the TV and before long the room was louder than ever.

"I'm. Just. Trying. To. Tell. You. That. I. Don't. Want. You. To. Leave. Walter!" Elizabeth hollered over the noise from the game. "That's all."

"I understand that, honey. That's what *you* want. But what about what I want?"

Oh boy.

"I care very much about what you want, Walter." Her expression tightened. "Always have. I'm only saying that the timing stinks. This is completely unfair of the publishing house to expect this of you right now."

"They are trying to give me an opportunity to sell books, Elizabeth. The more books I sell, the brighter our future will be. You do see that, don't you?"

"I see that you're not understanding me at all. For a man who knows so much about psychology, you can't seem to figure me out to save your life."

Oh boy, oh boy.

Did this room have an emergency exit?

She took a long slow breath and said nothing. Pop watched the game as if none of this was happening right in front of him. For the first time, I felt genuinely sorry for Walter. He said nothing. Absolutely nothing.

After a moment's pause, Elizabeth looked his way. "Do

you remember that scene in *To Kill A Mockingbird*, where Atticus was appointed by the judge to defend Tom Robinson, a man falsely accused?"

"Elizabeth are you really comparing our situation to the social injustices of the south during the Great Depression?"

"This is a little depressing," my father piped up. "Do you think Rosa's done with that lasagna yet, Bella?"

I sighed.

Elizabeth's tone grew more intense. "I'm just saying that some things aren't fair."

"Then just say some things aren't fair and leave it at that." Walter closed his eyes, as if trying to drown all of this out.

She sniffled and her eyes misted over. "Some. Things. Aren't. Fair!"

"What's not fair, honey?" Aunt Rosa entered the room, wiping her hands on her apron. "Have we run out of nuts?"

My father snorted. "Hardly."

"Well, the lasagna's ready. So are the garlic knots. They just came out of the oven."

"You just haven't lived till you've tasted Rosa's Garlic Knots, y'all." D.J.'s voice sounded from the foyer. "C'mon into the dining room while they're still hot."

Walter rose and extended his hand. Elizabeth took it. They followed on my heels to the dining room, where we all took our seats at the oversized table.

"Smells really good." Walter offered a weak smile. "Can't wait."

Uncle Laz said the blessing and then we dove in.

We were doing just fine. . .until Earline asked how the wedding plans were coming. Elizabeth ended up in tears.

"W-What did I say?" Earline looked at me, alarmed.

"You said nothing." Dwayne's father extended his hand.

"Could you pass the butter, hon?"

"But, I must've said *something*." Earline passed the butter, but couldn't stop staring at Elizabeth. "The poor girl's in tears."

Elizabeth sniffled. "I know what you're going to say, Walter. You're going to say that we should talk about this tomorrow. You always say we should talk about *everything* tomorrow. But tomorrow will be too late. You're leaving in the morning." She put her fork down and stared at him. "Tara's burning, Walter. It's going up in flames. We've got to stop the fire before we end up in ashes."

"Wait. . .what's burning?" Rosa looked up, clearly perplexed.

"Tara? Who's Tara?" Uncle Laz asked.

"*Gone with the Wind*. I'm referencing the fire scene." Elizabeth groaned. "Don't *any* of you read the classics? Tara went up in flames."

"Flames!" Rosa sniffed the air and then jumped up. "The brownies! I left them in the oven too long!"

Thank goodness, Rosa made it to the kitchen before the brownies burned to a crisp. I couldn't remember the last time she'd ever burned anything. Looked like this wedding duo was having an effect on the whole family.

Rosa returned awhile later with the scorched brownies. I nibbled on one. D.J. sat across from me, giving me the evil eye. Well, not exactly the evil eye, but close. No doubt he'd fill my ears when we got in the car.

"I wonder who won the game?" Pop asked as he bit into one of the brownies.

This somehow led to a conversation about colleges.

Which somehow led Walter to tell us that he'd graduated from A&M.

Which somehow led Rosa and Laz to gush about his latest book.

Which somehow ended up with Elizabeth in a crummy mood.

When she finally dried her eyes, she looked Walter's way.

"There was an incredible poignant scene in *All Quiet on the Western Front* where a young soldier, still in his teens, shoots and kills an enemy soldier, a boy not much older than himself."

"Well, isn't this cheerful." Earline fanned herself with her napkin.

"The two boys have to spend the night in the trench."

"One dead, one alive?" My mother shivered. "Oh my."

"Yes. As the hours tick by, the boy who killed his enemy has plenty of time to reflect on his choices. He sees, probably for the first time in his young life, the effects of war on a ravaged soul."

"More brownies, anyone?" Aunt Rosa picked up the platter and attempted to pass it Elizabeth's way.

"There are so many lessons to be learned from this story." Elizabeth said. "Not the least of which is, we all make choices—some of them good, and some of them bad." She gave Walter the same evil eye D.J. had given me just moments before. "And the bad ones often have devastating long-term consequences."

The groom-to-be stopped eating his brownie, his eyes growing as wide as saucers.

In that moment, I learned everything I needed to know about Walter and Elizabeth—and none of it could be solved with a math equation. There would be no more adding or subtracting of points. He might have his issues, but this bride-to-be had quite a few, as well. And, if she didn't get her emotions under control, Tara very well might go up in flames, taking us all down with it.

Chapter Seven

WAR AND PEACE

Walter and Elizabeth headed out right after dinner to head back to Houston. I'd never been so happy to see a bride and groom-to-be leave in all my years as a wedding planner.

Now, to get myself back in the good graces of my family. Hopefully they wouldn't kill me for ruining what should've been a perfectly lovely night.

I headed into the living room to discover everyone seated in front of the TV. Only, the TV wasn't on. They looked pretty glazed over, to be honest. The first comment came from D.J.'s dad.

"Well, that was different."

"That gal is an emotional mess, isn't she?" Earline fanned herself again.

"Someone needs to teach that psychologist-fellow how to speak to a woman so that she feels secure in herself." Mama clucked her tongue. "That poor, poor bride."

"Poor bride?" Laz snorted. "Really? She's a nightmare. Who would want to marry a woman who carried on like that? I say, run. . .as fast and as far as you can."

This started a lengthy—and very, very loud—

conversation, in which the various attendees stated a variety of opinions about whether or not Elizabeth and Walter were even ready for marriage in the first place. Ugh. How did we get here, and how could I get us out?

I kept a watchful eye on D.J., who never said a word. Oh, I could tell he wanted to, especially when my dad went off on a tangent about Walter being a know-it-all. Ack.

The noise continued to rise as the women turned on the men, arguing about who was more to blame—the bride or the groom.

I turned to face D.J., more alarmed than I'd been all day long.

"Whoa, whoa, whoa!" My husband put his hand up. "Hang on just a doggone minute, folks." When they didn't stop arguing, he let out a shrill whistle, one of those 'two fingers in the mouth' ones. That certainly put a stop to the debate.

"Did you have to go and do that, D.J.?" Earline put her fingers in her ears.

"I think I've just lost what was left of my hearing." Dwayne Sr. rubbed at his ears with his palms.

"Yes, I had to do that. Someone had to put a stop to this madness." D.J. paced the room. "Do you hear yourselves?" When no one responded, he added, "Do you?"

"We're just sharing our opinions, D.J.," Mama said. "Nothing wrong with that."

"Nothing wrong with that?" He shook his head. "Half of you just went on and on about how crazy and inappropriate this psychologist-guy is, and how emotional the bride is." He turned to face his father. "What was it you just called him, Dad?"

"I. . .well. . ." Mr. Neeley's face turned red.

" And what did you say about him, Mama?"

Earline offered a sheepish grin. "I might've said he needed to be taken out behind the woodshed and whupped for not making his woman feel secure in herself. Something like that."

"Right. And you, Laz? Didn't I just hear you say something derogatory about Elizabeth?"

Laz rolled his eyes. "That woman is a piece of work. She needs someone to give her what-for and tell her to get over herself."

"She's just hurting inside," Mama countered. "As are so many women when they don't feel loved."

"Which begs the question: Isn't this fella supposed to be good at what he does?" Earline rolled her eyes. "Sounds like he needs to go back to school to me."

"Okay, enough already." D.J. groaned. Loudly. "Listen to yourselves. Do you really hear what you're saying?"

"I don't get your point, D.J." Rosa looked perplexed. "You don't think we have a right to voice an opinion about someone who thinks he's always right?"

"You don't think we need to be honest about a bride who's over the top?" Dwayne added.

"I'm not saying you don't have a right, I'm just saying it's. . ." D.J. squinted. "Ironic."

"Ironic, how?" Earline asked.

He turned to face her. "Mama, did you or did you not just tell Bubba two days ago that he and Jenna needed to have two more children?"

She blanched. "Well, I might've said something to that effect, but—"

"And I'm pretty sure you told me just tonight that we need to move to Splendora and raise our children in the country."

"Sure. But I don't get your point."

"Point is, everyone in this family—he pointed to all in attendance—is guilty of thinking they're right. And everyone in this room has played psychologist in the lives of everyone else in this room. And, hold onto your hats, folks—most of you have had emotional outbursts like the bride did tonight." He put his hands up in the air. "Shocker, I know."

This, of course, started a completely different debate.

D.J. whistled again. "Remember that time you almost sued your neighbors, Mr. Rossi?"

My pop cleared his throat.

"And remember that time you threatened to take Mayor Deets to court, Dad?" He looked at his father.

"That was a long time ago, son. Tommy Deets and I are friends now."

"I know, but you get my point. We all like to think we know best. Just like that Walter fella. And there's never been a shortage of opinions in this family." He paused and looked around. "Am I right?"

A few mumbled, "Yeah" and "You're right about that."

"I'm just saying, Walter is trained. He has years of experience behind him."

"I've got experience telling folks what to do, too," Earline said. "Think they'll give me a paycheck like his?"

"He's got the PhD behind his name, Mama. He studied for years."

"Book-smarts don't give a fella the right to tell others how to live."

"Neither does living in a family, but we all do it, anyway." D.J. put his hands on his hips. "Get my point?"

They got it, all right. In fact, they got it so well that they started squabbling. Again. Before long, Mama was arguing that she never ever told others how to live their lives. And Pop? He went off on a tangent about the time Mama insisted he stop wearing his jockey shorts around the house.

I had to interject at this point. "Stop, everyone." They didn't listen, so I yelled, "Stop it, already!"

The bickering came to an abrupt halt. "D.J.'s right, whether we want to admit it or not. We're all too free with our opinions. I'll be the first to say so. But I've been on the receiving end a lot lately, and I have to say, it stings."

"What do you mean, Bella?" Mama took a couple of steps in my direction. "Who hurt my girl?" Her gaze narrowed as she took in everyone else in the room.

"*You*, Mama." I gave her a knowing look. "Did you or did you not tell me that I need to give up my work at the wedding facility?"

She gave me a wide-eyed stare. "I didn't say give it up, exactly. I just said that you're expecting baby number five now, and you'll need to spend more time at home."

"Which I already plan to do, by the way, but did anyone think to ask me about that?" I shook my head. "No. Why would you ask when you could tell me what to do?"

"Well, Bella, I. . ." Mama's words drifted off.

This led Pop to tell a story about what a know-it-all Mama was.

"Pop." I shook my head as he looked my way. "Didn't you tell D.J. just last week that he needed to go back to driving school to learn how to handle a vehicle?"

"I never meant anything by that, Bella." Pop shifted his gaze to D.J. and then shrugged.

"Sounds like you folks have a lot of problems." Laz leaned back against the sofa.

Rosa glared at my uncle. "Now, wait a minute, Lazarro

Rossi. If there was ever a man who loved to tell others how to live—what to do, what to eat, what to wear, how to cook—it was you."

"Me?" His voice elevated and even cracked a little. "Me? Woman, you blame me for telling others how to cook, when you won't even allow half the family in that kitchen of yours because you're afraid they'll mess up your food?"

"Is that why you don't like me to come in the kitchen, Rosa?" Mama's eyes filled with tears. "I knew you didn't care for my cooking, but I try. I really try."

I gave D.J. an imploring "See what you've started?" look.

The poor fella looked panicked.

We somehow got the natives calmed down and I decided we'd better head home. I whispered up a prayer of thanks that my children had missed all of this. How traumatized they would have been to hear their elders bickering.

I did my best to say a calm, peaceful 'goodnight' to my family members, then we headed out of the front door. When we got to the veranda, I turned to face my husband, ready to give him a piece of my mind for getting everyone so riled up. Just as I prepared myself to say something—anything—he sighed and slipped his arm around my shoulders. "Don't say it, Bella. Don't say it."

Okay, then. I'd be the only one in the Rossi-Neeley clan who managed to keep her opinions to herself.

Maybe.

When we reached the front steps, D.J.'s phone beeped. He pulled it out of his back pocket and opened a text message. His expression changed immediately.

"Everything okay?" I asked.

"Yeah." A smile lit his face. "Everything's *very* okay." He turned the phone around to reveal a picture of Goldie with a passel of pups nestled against her.

"Look who decided to come a little early." He gave me a pleading look.

In that moment, I knew I had to do the right thing. There would be no arguments with D.J. about this. I wouldn't be a know-it-all, giving him a thousand excuses why this wouldn't work. Instead, I threw my arms around my honey's neck and said, "Well? What are we going to name him?"

Chapter Eight

SENSE AND SENSIBILITY

The following afternoon, just after church, I received an apology call from Elizabeth. I'd somehow sensed it would be coming—D.J. and I had even taken bets on it—but I hadn't prepared myself for what she might say.

D.J. took the children upstairs for their naps and I settled down onto our sofa to chat with her.

"I don't know what came over me, Bella." She released a slow sigh. "I truly don't. I rarely let my emotions get out of control like that, at least not in front of people."

I somehow doubted that, but didn't say so.

"W-Will you forgive me?"

"Of course."

"I'm not crazy. I need you to know that." She paused. "I mean, I'm eccentric. I love good books. Lots and lots of books. But that doesn't make me crazy. Does it?"

"Of course not."

"And I love Walter. I really, really do. He loves me too, Bella."

"I never doubted it."

"We're probably not your average wedding couple."

That would be putting it mildly.

"And we might show our love differently than most. But I can promise you this: we're head-over-heels, can't-walk-straight in love. And he's promised me that everything will work out. We'll get married the week after he gets back in town and we'll live happily ever after."

"That's the dream of every bride."

"Especially one as addicted to stories as I am." She giggled, her mood now lighter than before.

"I know I drive people crazy with my literature analogies." She sighed. "Trust me, plenty of people have told me. But that's just how my mind works. I love stories. I find myself in them all the time. Take *Little Women*, for instance. I've always connected to Jo."

"That's funny," I added. "I always felt like Meg, the oldest sister."

"See? Just goes to prove that stories compel us to learn more about ourselves. My favorite, of course, is *Pride and Prejudice*. It's just so. . .so. . ." She stopped talking and I wondered if I'd lost her. "It's so relatable. We all struggle with issues of pride. I know people think Walter does, but I do, too. If you think about it, even insecurity is a form of pride. I mean, anything that forces me to spend too much time focused on myself is pride. You know? That's really what happened yesterday. We were both having a *Pride and Prejudice* day. That's not an excuse, by the way. Just an explanation."

"Never thought about it like that before. And to be perfectly honest, I haven't read *Pride and Prejudice*. I've seen the movie—not the really long one. Never had time for that. But I saw the one that came out a few years ago."

"Bella, you have to read the book. It's so much better than any movie could ever be. Promise you will."

"I will do my best."

"But you have read Walter's new book, right?"

Ack. I'd been dreading this question.

"Oh, Bella," she said after the silence between us grew uncomfortable. "You should. It's really pretty amazing."

Time to come clean. "Elizabeth, when I first read the title: *I'm Okay, You Need Work*. . .it just kind of threw me a little."

She laughed. "You do know the title is just a hook, right?"

"A hook?" What did she mean by that?

"Sure. Something to grab the reader and pull him in. A little reverse psychology, as it were. The principles inside the book are all about how we—and by we, I mean all of us—are inclined to think that others are the ones who need to change. But the truth is, we have to face facts. It starts with us. Kind of like what happened yesterday. I had expectations of Walter. He had expectations of me. But it didn't take me long to see that I was the one who was driving that train last night, and I very nearly derailed us. When I got home last night I picked up the book and read chapter four again. Totally transformed my thinking."

"So, you're telling me the book is the opposite of the title?"

"Yep. But people buy the book because they think Walter is going to teach them how to change others. In essence, the whole thing is just a revelation about how we need to be agents of change for ourselves, first."

"Wow."

"Mm-hmm. He's a busy man, and he's overwhelmed with his work, but Walter's such a great guy, Bella. It's hard to tell at times, but he really is."

Maybe I'd been wrong about him. Maybe we all had.

"He's the kindest man I know. He'd give the shirt off his

back to help others. Last week a woman called in to his show and told him about her son, who has Cerebral Palsy and needs a new wheelchair. She was really calling to talk about how she communicates with her son, but Walter heard much more than that. He heard her say that she's pretty much on her own and has great financial needs. So, you know what my Walter did?"

"What?"

"He set up a caregiver to go into the woman's home to help with the little boy. And he hired a friend of his—an amazing therapist who specializes in kids with neuromuscular issues—to work with the little boy's speech. But the best part is, he arranged for the mother and son to go to Disneyworld for a full week."

"Wow."

"Yes, wow. Only, no one knows any of this. . .well, other than the two of us, and you're sworn to secrecy."

I put up two fingers as if taking the Girl Scout pledge. Then I realized no one could see me.

Except my son, who'd snuck down the stairs to avoid taking a nap. I gave Tres a little wink and he rushed to cuddle up next to me on the sofa.

"I won't tell a soul," I promised.

"Walter won't, either," Elizabeth said. "He never brags on himself, but that's just one of a hundred stories I could tell you. I'm not saying he's a rich man, but what he has, he shares. And the pool of people he works with? They're happy to go along with what he asks of them because they see his heart, his *true* heart. So, when I said earlier that Walter has a way of winning people over to his way of thinking, I didn't mean it in a bad way. He's persuasive, but it's always for the greater good."

"Wow." I hardly knew what to say in response to all of

this.

"One more thing, Bella, and this is where my advice ends."

"What's that?"

"You really need to read more."

"I know, I know. But I have four kids, Elizabeth, with one more on the way. Who has time to read?"

"Make the time. I promise, it will revolutionize your life. Go back through the classics, maybe one a month. Before long you'll be so enamored with the stories that you won't be able to put them down."

I doubted it, but wouldn't tell her that. "You know," I said after a moment's pause, "I never thought about it before, but I guess that's one reason I love reading the stories in the Old Testament so much. I see myself in so many of them."

"That's good story-telling right there." She laughed. "Then again, I guess you could say God is the ultimate author."

"Right? But I never thought about what effort he put into writing down those real-life stories in a way that we could relate to today. I mean, half the time I'm in the pit with Joseph. The other half I'm falling asleep at the wheel, like the disciples in the garden. Sometimes I'm Martha, working in a frenzy, and other times I'm Mary, quiet and still at his feet."

"The good news is, there's enough reading material there for the rest of your life. And it's funny you should mention the story of the disciples in the garden. That's the Bible story I most relate to."

"Really?"

"You don't know my past, Bella. The reason I lost myself in stories, even as a kid, was because of horrible abuse. The things that were done to me. . ." Her voice cracked. "Well, no child should have to endure."

"Oh, Elizabeth, I'm so sorry."

She paused and I could almost envision her swiping her eyes with the back of her hand, as she so often did. "As a kid I would just lose myself in novels to escape my reality. Those characters were bold. They were brave. They were strong. In a thousand ways they gave me hope."

"Nothing wrong with that," I said.

"No. Nothing wrong with that. I love fiction. But I love a real story even more, which is why the story of Jesus resonated with me so deeply, starting with what he went through in the garden. I didn't grow up in church. I didn't know anything about the gospels or even who Jesus really was. The only time I heard his name was when my dad was swearing at me." She paused. "But I had a good friend, a girl in my 10th grade class, who recommended what she called the greatest story on earth. She challenged me to read the gospel of John. . .and I did it just to shut her up, if you want the truth."

"Wow, Elizabeth. So, what happened?"

"Great writing in that book," she said. "I could spend all day talking to you about the characterization, the tone, the style. But what really hit me was the part where Jesus chose to forgive those who should have stuck by him, even those who abused him. Even in the worst pain, hanging on the cross, his words were laced with compassion and forgiveness. In that moment, I found myself in the story. And it changed me forever."

Okay, now we were both in tears.

"I *know* I'm not your typical bride, Bella. And I'm sorry that I've made things harder on you and your family than they needed to be."

"All is forgiven, girl."

"Thank you. Truth is, I've had so many hard reality checks in my life that I'm due a few happily-ever-afters. And even though Walter doesn't always seem like the literary hero-type, he's the Mr. Darcy to my Elizabeth." She paused and then smiled. "That's the first time I've caught the irony of that. I guess I really am Elizabeth Bennett, after all."

This led to another round of praises for *Pride and Prejudice*. By the time we ended the call, she'd made me promise I would read it. I agreed.

When we hung up, I rose from the sofa and snagged my laptop from my office. When I returned to the living room, Tres looked up at me.

"Whatcha doin', Mommy?" he asked.

"Oh, just thought I'd order something online, that's all."

"A present? For me?"

I smiled as I scooted back into my spot on the sofa next to him. "No, son. A present for mommy."

I opened my laptop and went straight to Amazon, where I browsed the classics with my now-dozing son at my side. Might as well purchase a few. Twenty minutes and ten novels later, I'd placed my order. Would I find myself in the same stories that had captivated Elizabeth? Only time would tell. But, for the first time in forever, I was ready to find out.

Chapter Nine

TENDER IS THE NIGHT

The second Saturday in November dawned bright and clear, the air crisp and cool. I peeked out of my bedroom window, started to see the leaves on the trees were finally changing. Wow. Looked like Elizabeth and Walter—who had recently returned from his book tour—would have their fall wedding after all.

I raced through the morning, fixing breakfast for the kids, dressing them for the day, and then kissing them goodbye when Sophia arrived to watch them.

This is the big day!

Oh boy.

I arrived at the wedding facility mid-morning, ready to get to work. D.J. sauntered in behind me, dragging in one of the faux bookshelves, which looked so much like the real deal I felt myself wanting to pull the books down and read them.

Mama, Rosa and I worked on the chapel while D.J. and Pop did their thing in the reception hall. Afterwards, I went to check on Cassia, who was setting up centerpieces on the tablecloth covered reception tables. I couldn't help but gasp when I saw them.

"Oh, Cassia! Those are perfect!"

"Thanks." She turned to face me, a broad smile on her face. "All of the old books belong to Elizabeth. She-she-she—achoo!" Cassia sneezed. "Sorry, I've been doing that ever since she brought them to me. I dusted them off, but. . .wow."

"Well, they're perfect in little stacks like that. And I love the fall flowers and little pumpkins. Just right with those old-fashioned looking book covers."

"Trust me, she worked hard to pick out books with corresponding color covers. That girl's on the ball."

"She is, for sure."

At two o'clock, Scarlet arrived with the cake. She'd brought the tiers in separate boxes, so I didn't get the full effect until after the whole thing was put together. I had to smile when I saw how lovely and wedding-like the cake looked. Sure, the bottom tier looked like a little library, what with all of the fondant book spines in their various fall colors. And yes, Walter's book took the spot of honor on the top tier. But the cake—straight and level—had no *Alice in Wonderland* feel to it at all. Seemed just perfect for this couple, and all the more when I saw Scarlet add the vibrant fall flowers to trim in out. Afterwards, she stepped back.

"What do you think, Bella?"

I sighed. "Scarlet, I don't know how you did it, but you've captured both of them—without all the drama."

We both laughed.

"I love how it matches the bookshelves D.J. made." She gestured to the far side of the room, complete with library-esque shelving, antique loveseats, and old-fashioned reading chairs. "This is really something, Bella. Different from anything you've done before."

"I know, and I love it. The people from Stages Event

Planning were here all morning. We just gave them instructions. And approximately forty Pinterest pictures. I think they're used to that, though."

"Do you think Walter will like it?"

"He will love it. But, honestly? He's still floating on Cloud 9. Did you hear that his book hit the New York Times bestseller list a couple of days ago, thanks to that book tour of his?"

"I'm not surprised." She released a little sigh. "I *loved* that book. So great."

"I know, right? Kind of caught me off-guard, but I loved it, too. Even D.J. said it was spot-on, and he's not a lets-go-to-counseling kind of guy."

"I appreciated how Walter turned everything around and laid the need for change on the reader, not the other person." Scarlet's nose wrinkled. "Between you and me, I've spent a lot of years trying to tweak your brother. Armando has little habits that drive me insane. But, Walter's book convinced me that I need to work on myself first. . .and that's a good thing. You know?"

"I do know."

We both stood back and looked at the room in stillness for a moment.

And then I heard the bride's voice. "Oh, Bella!"

I turned to discover she'd entered with her bridesmaids. Her makeup and hair were already done, but she wore jeans and a button-up shirt. The bridesmaids began to carry on the minute they saw the room. I didn't blame them. And Elizabeth? She looked like she might just cry.

"No, no, no, no, no!" I exclaimed. "Don't ruin your makeup."

"It's just so. . .so. . .perfect!" Her gaze traveled the length of the room from right to left. "I feel like I've walked into the Rosenberg library in autumn, when it's all decked out for the season. Only, of course, it's prettier than that." She shifted her gaze. "And that cake! Oh, Scarlet!" At this point a few tears brimmed her mascara-covered lashes. "It's like you saw right inside my head."

"Actually, she showed me approximately thirty Pinterest pictures," Scarlet whispered in my ear.

I got the bridal party calmed down and pointed them in the direction of the changing room.

By five o'clock, the wedding was in full swing. We managed to squeeze a larger-than-expected number of guests into the chapel and I went to find the caterer to make sure we wouldn't run out of food. Turned out, he'd prepared more than necessary, thank goodness.

I stood at the back of the chapel and watched as Walter and Elizabeth said their I Do's. In that moment, as I heard the emotion in both of their voices, I was reminded of that awful evening at my parents' house. If you had asked me then, I would've said these two were the least likely to survive their marriage. But, after reading Walter's book, after hearing Elizabeth's impassioned speech about her husband-to-be's good traits, I'd had time to reflect and re-think.

All couples faced differences of opinion.

All couples had their problems.

And all couples could probably stand to have a few hours of counseling once in a while.

My thoughts shifted to D.J., who was still in the reception hall, probably nibbling on some Turkish Delight, whatever that was. He was about as close to perfect as he could possibly be, and yet he'd still chosen me—a chaotic, loud, A.D.D.-ish girl who spent way too many hours with her crazy family. Oh, how

I loved my fella.

My gaze shifted back to the bride and groom as they kissed for the first time as man and wife. As they began their trek down the aisle, I flew into wedding planner gear once again.

A few minutes later, we were ushering guests into the reception hall. Many of them pulled out their cell phones and started taking pictures of the décor. They oohed and aahed with delight, and several headed right for the love seats and reading chairs. A handful even looked over the stacks of books on the tables to see which titles Elizabeth had strategically chosen.

I'd never thought to do that, but even the individual books, themselves, were a direct reflection of what she loved.

What she loved.

I couldn't help but get misty-eyed as the bridal party made their way in. How happy Elizabeth looked on her groom's arm. And how peaceful he appeared as he leaned over to give her a kiss.

The reception seemed to buzz by, but I loved every second. In fact, I'd have to rate this wedding in my top ten of all time, not just because I'd taken the time to figure out the bride and groom, but because I saw them—their story—in every detail.

Every story.

We all had one, didn't we?

The evening's events wrapped up at eight o'clock, just as the limo pulled up to usher the bride and groom to their honeymoon suite at The Tremont. Just before Elizabeth rushed out on her groom's arm, she approached me. I was standing with my family in the kitchen, ready to get to work, pulling down the décor and putting the room back together.

"How can I ever thank you enough, Bella?" She gave me a hug and then faced my family. "I'm so grateful for all of you."

"You're so welcome." I returned her hug and then took a step back. "I think it came off beautifully."

"Mm-hmm." She paused and I could see the contentment in her eyes. "It's the pearl of great price."

"I'm sorry, what?"

"Oh, you know." Elizabeth sighed as she looked around the reception hall one last time. "John Steinbeck's classic, *The Pearl*. It's about a man who gains everything, only to lose his soul. Oh, and his child. The baby died. Scorpion bite."

Mama shivered. "Remind me never to read that book."

"For pity's sake." Rosa looked at my uncle. "That's worse than that television show you tried to make me watch the other night, Laz. What was it called, again?"

"Survivor?"

"Yes, *Survivor*. But there were no scorpions." Her nose wrinkled. "I do think that one of the contestants wore pearls, though, now that I think of it. The others made fun of her for getting dolled up like that out in the wilderness." Off Rosa went on a tangent. I could tell she'd completely lost Elizabeth. I pulled the new bride aside and gave her a warm hug.

"Everything was gorgeous, Elizabeth. You've made a believer out of me. And you won't believe it, but I've started reading again. I finished *Little Women* a few days ago and I'm over halfway through *Pride and Prejudice*."

"Oh, Bella, good!" She gave my hand a squeeze. "Remember what I said. Look for yourself in the story. That's the point of good writing, to draw you in."

"I will, I promise."

Several minutes later, with the bridal family gone and the

guests headed out to their cars, the whole Rossi family worked together, as we so often did, to clean up the reception hall. I hated to pull down the bookshelves because I found myself drawn to them. Apparently Laz liked them, too. He balked when D.J. began to disassemble them.

"I guess this would be as good a time as any to tell you folks something." Laz spoke above the whirring of D.J.'s drill. "I'm going back to college."

"What?" Rosa turned his way and clamped a hand over her mouth.

"But you're an old married man now, Laz," Pop said. "What's the point? You've got a great business. You've even got your own show on The Food Network. What more could a fella want?"

"A few letters behind his name, that's what." Laz flashed a broad smile. "Look, I barely finished high school. Never had the opportunity to do anything beyond that. But I figure it's never too late. Walter convinced me I could do it, and I'd sure like to try. Hope I have your support, everyone."

He had our support, all right. The family gathered around him, all talking at once. They left the messy room to clean itself as they took seats at the tables to chat about Laz's decision.

D.J. and I looked on from a distance as we continued our work.

"There's always tomorrow. We can think about cleaning up then, I suppose."

"*Gone with the Wind*," I said, and then laughed. "Scarlett O'Hara was always putting things off till tomorrow when she didn't want to deal with them today."

D.J. stopped working and slipped his arm around my shoulder. "I dare say, Elizabeth is rubbing off on you."

"Yep. And I guess that's a good thing." My hand went to my belly as the baby fluttered. Off in the distance, my family carried on with great abandon, their volume rising more and more with each syllable spoken.

They were crazy.

They were loud.

They were nuts at times.

But, they were mine.

Oh boy.

"One thing's for sure," I whispered in D.J.'s ear. "Even if I never read another book, I'll have plenty of story, right in front of me."

"And *what* a story it is," he said. . .and then kissed me.

Chapter Ten

THE PEARL

A couple of days after the wedding I found myself enamored with Mr. Darcy and Elizabeth Bennett. I flipped through the pages of *Pride and Prejudice* in rapid succession, growing more and more intrigued with where the story was taking me. Sure, I'd seen the movie, but. . .the book! Oh, nothing compared.

I managed to sneak in several hours of reading with the older two kids in school, but once they arrived home, I had to lay down the book. Of course, I had to fix dinner and give the kids their baths, but I found myself wanting to get back to those final chapters.

D.J., God bless him, got the kids settled into bed for the night so that I could wrap up the story. Half an hour later, while he showered and dressed for bed, I read the final page.

Oh, how it made my heart sing. Oh, if only life really worked out like it did in the chapters of this amazing tale. Wouldn't that be lovely?

I put the book on the bedside table, blissfully content.

"All done?" D.J. asked. He came out of the bathroom dressed in pajama pants, but no shirt.

Mr. Darcy's got nothing on you, fella.

I almost spoke the words aloud but stopped myself. No point in embarrassing my sweetie.

"Mm-hmm. Loved it. Every word."

"Did anyone get shot?"

"No, silly." I gestured for him to join me in bed. "It was a romance. *Pride and Prejudice*."

"People get shot in romance stories all the time. Don't you watch TV?" He climbed into the bed and leaned back against his pillows.

"Sure, but not this one. It was about a guy who was kind of in love with this woman who didn't know that she loved him too, only she did, but she was too prejudiced to see it, and he was too prideful to admit it, so it took awhile to admit what they were really feeling."

"And they shot each other in the end?" He quirked a brow.

I fought the temptation to throw my pillow at him. "No. I told you, there were no shootings."

"Ah." D.J. shrugged. "No offense, but it sounds a little boring."

"D.J., you know nothing about romances."

"Oh, no?" His eyebrows elevated mischievously. "Wanna bet?"

Seconds later, his kisses had me swooning, and all the more as the moved to my neck. A delicious shiver ran through me. He gave me a kiss so passionate that I felt sure even Jane Austen would've blushed.

Afterward, D.J. leaned back on his pillow and gave me a knowing look. "You were saying?"

A giggle escaped. "I was saying that you put Mr. Darcy to shame."

"No idea who this Darcy fellow is, but you put him right

out of your head, Bella. He can't have you. You tell him to skedaddle."

"Yes, Sir. I'll tell him to skedaddle." I paused. "I didn't realize how much I enjoyed reading, D.J. Is that weird?"

"Not weird at all. You're just. . .busy."

"I am. Very. But things are slowing down, and I'm thinking that's a good thing."

"Yep," he drawled.

"When we start drawing up plans for a new house, will you add a library?"

"A library?" He chuckled. "How about if we just call it your office? You can fill the shelves with anything you like."

"Sounds perfect." I snuggled up against him. "Can I ask you a question?"

"Shore," he drawled. "Ask me anything you like, Bella-Bambina."

"Do you like our story?"

"Like our story?" He paused and gave me a comical look. "We have a story?"

"Sure. The story of us. You. Me. The kids."

"And Harley." He looked my way and smiled.

"Harley?"

"The puppy. He's almost five weeks old now, Bella. It won't be long before he's part of the family. By Christmas, anyway."

"You named him without me?"

"The kids named him. Okay, they might've had a little help from me. But we think it fits him. You okay with that?"

"As long as you let me help name this little one." I ran my palm across my belly and felt a fluttering like angel wings.

"You've got a deal. We'll call him Fido."

I slapped myself on the forehead.

"Kidding, Bella. Kidding." D.J. gave me another kiss.

"Okay, so. . .You. Me. The kids. Harley. Do you like our story?" I asked once more.

His eyes filled with tears so quickly that it caught me by surprise. D.J. pulled me close and planted several kisses in my hair. "Bella, I *love* our story. There's never been one finer. It's a real page-turner—up one minute, down the next, messes in the living room, chaos in the kitchen. We're a regular best-seller."

"Elizabeth says she always finds herself in the novels she reads. But I think it's the other way around with us. What we've got—" A lump rose in my throat and I did my best to push it down. "What we've got is so special that it trumps any story in a book."

"Oh, I don't know. Maybe one day someone will write about us." D.J. kissed my cheek. "Maybe we'll become famous, just like Miss Darcy and Mr. Bennett."

"Their names were Elizabeth Bennett and Mr. Darcy.

"Whatever. Point is, we've got enough stories to keep folks laughing for years. You know?"

"True, that. But heaven help the poor person who chooses to pen our tale. She'd certainly have her hands full, trying to keep up with the Rossi's, the Neeleys and all of those Splendora folks."

I got tired, just thinking about it.

Still, D.J. was right. We had enough stories to fill dozens of books. Not that our tale had come to an end yet. Not even close. I still had a little one to bring into this world, after all. And a new dog to tend to. And a new house to design. And we still had to raise this brood of ours, in the very center of the craziest—and sweetest—family on Galveston Island.

And while we were at it, I might just take a little break

from wedding planning. Oh, not give it up completely. I'd still take on an occasional shindig, like the one coming up in January.

But after that? Well, maybe I'd just settle into my storybook life with my hunky hero and see where the plotline took us.

A NOTE FROM THE AUTHOR

Thank you for reading *The Tender Trap*. I hope you enjoyed traveling back to Galveston with Bella for this bookish ceremony.

I so enjoyed writing this story, particularly because it gave me the opportunity to revisit some of my favorite pieces of classic literature. Like Elizabeth, I love *Little Women*! It's my very favorite.

There's ONE more story coming around the bend for Bella. Stay tuned for a winter novella titled *Return to Me*, which will celebrate the birth of Bella and D.J.'s fifth (and final) child. I can't wait to share that story!

Thanks again for reading. I'm always delighted to reveal more of Bella's world to some of my favorite people, my precious readers.

HAVE YOU READ ALL THE BELLA NOVELLAS?

Once Upon a Moonlight Night (A Winter Wonderland Wedding)
Tea for Two (A Victorian Valentine's Day Ceremony)
Pennies from Heaven (A Springtime Garden Ceremony)
That Lucky Old Sun (A Galveston Beach Ceremony)
The Tender Trap (An Autumn Shabby Chic Ceremony)
That's Life! (Bella's final story)

HAVE YOU READ THE BOOKS THAT STARTED IT ALL?

THE CLUB WED SERIES:
Fools Rush In
Swinging on a Star
It Had to be You

THE BACKSTAGE PASS SERIES:
Stars Collide
Hello Hollywood
The Director's Cut

THE WEDDINGS BY DESIGN SERIES
Picture Perfect
The Icing on the Cake
The Dream Dress
A Bouquet of Love

ABOUT THE AUTHOR

Award-winning author Janice Thompson got her start in the industry writing screenplays and musical comedies for the stage. Janice has published over 100 books for the Christian market, crossing genre lines to write cozy mysteries, historicals, romances, nonfiction books, devotionals, children's books and more. She particularly enjoys writing light-hearted, comedic tales because she enjoys making readers laugh. Janice is passionate about her faith and does all she can to share the joy of the Lord with others, which is why she particularly enjoys writing. Her tagline, "Love, Laughter, and Happily Ever Afters!" sums up her take on life.

Janice lives in Spring, Texas, where she leads a rich life with her family, a host of writing friends, and two mischievous dachshunds. When she's not busy writing or playing with her eight grandchildren, she can be found in the kitchen, baking specialty cakes and cookies for friends and loved ones. No matter what Janice is cooking up—books, cakes, cookies or mischief—she does her best to keep the Lord at the center of it all. You can find out more about this wacky author at www.janiceathompson.com. Sign up for Janice's Newsletter to learn about all of her upcoming projects and future books in the series. As a thank you from Janice you will receive a free copy of her cookbook when you sign up.

ACKNOWLEDGMENTS

I'm so grateful to the following:

My Dream Team: What an amazing group of readers and friends you are! I could never publish a book without you! (Truly!) Thanks for proofing my story and for helping with cover ideas. You gals are the best!

The MacGregor Literary Agency: Thank you for your undying support, no matter which publishing route I choose.

Made in the USA
Middletown, DE
13 November 2023

42585718R00052